N No ...ges

Ann Pilling

Illustrated by
JOLYNE KNOX
HEINEMANN · LONDON

for the Pattinson Family,
with love

William Heinemann Ltd
10 Upper Grosvenor Street, London W1X 9PA

LONDON · MELBOURNE · TORONTO
JOHANNESBURG · AUCKLAND

First published 1986
Reprinted 1987
Text © Ann Pilling 1986
Illustrations © Jolyne Knox 1986

A school pack of BANANA BOOKS 13–18 is
available from Heinemann Educational Books
ISBN 0 435 00102 7

434 93039 3
Printed in Hong Kong by
Imago Publishing Ltd

The Funny Friendship

THE BOY IN this story is called Lugsy
Malone. His real name was George
but he was always getting terrible
knots in his hair. 'Lugs' his grandma
called them.

You couldn't find anything at
George's house. He had six little
brothers and sisters and the place was
a tip. In the mornings he was lucky if
he found a sweater and a pair of
trousers, and as for combs . . . there
just weren't any.

So he always had 'lugs' and his hair used to stick out in a big black frizz, as if it had been given an electric shock. Everyone called him Lugsy.

He got the name when a film came round, about a gang of children. They had 'splurge guns' that spattered the Baddies with custard, and the leader of the gang was called Bugsy, Bugsy Malone.

The girl who dreamed up the nickname was a girl called Monica Teesdale and she was his best friend in 3.S. Lugsy was skinny and small, with his frizzy electric hair, and Monica was big and fat with a round pink face. She had strange hair too, a great blonde busby, a bit like a guardsman's hat. Perched right on top, her school beret looked like a pimple sitting on a mountain.

Lugsy and Monica were friends for two reasons. *One*: they were both a bit funny-looking, and *Two*: they both had secret vices.

Monica's secret vice was eating. Her mum and dad ran a health shop in the town centre, and at home she was given lots of nuts and raw carrot, and sticky brown bread with treacle in it.

3

But she didn't really like health food. Whenever she could she swapped her packed lunch for Lugsy's – a crunchy oat bar in exchange for two jam sandwiches, and a big red apple in exchange for a packet of crisps. It suited Lugsy. They didn't have Monica's kind of food at his house.

She often brought oranges to school, but they always got her into trouble with Miss Gauntlet. The headmistress hated the smell, and she also hated litter. Monica was absent-minded, and she sometimes dropped the peel when she was busy talking to Lugsy. One morning Miss Gauntlet saw her.

Next day there was a blitz on litter.
A notice went up. '*Banned*: crisps,
bubble-gum, chocolate bars and
oranges.' The Head was having no
more peel in her clean playground.

Lugsy's secret vice was guns, and he had a big collection. His dad was in the Army and said that guns were no laughing matter, and should never be *pointed* at anybody.

'I agree,' said Lugsy meekly, and he never laughed, or pointed. They were only toys anyway, and most of the time he just looked at them. Guns were banned from school, along with bubble-gum and oranges.

Monica called Miss Gauntlet 'Stone Age Woman'. She didn't believe in modern things like TVs or pocket calculators. She only believed in Work, with a capital 'W', and the minute she arrived at Green End School she cut outings down to one a year, for each class.

By the time 3.S.'s turn came round Lugsy and Monica were fed up with waiting, and when they heard who was taking them they didn't want to go. It was Mr Simpkins, their class teacher, tall and thin, and looking like a long drink of water. He was so feeble he couldn't knock a fly off custard, not even a dead one.

'Clean hands, clean faces, packed lunches and school hats,' Miss Gauntlet bellowed at them, the day of the trip. 'No silly behaviour, no getting lost, no *guns* and no *oranges*.' She said the last bit very loudly.

No prizes for guessing who she was looking at.

Off to the Zoo

WHEN THE COACH came everybody tried to get on at once. 'Please don't *push*, 3.S.,' Mr Simpkins squeaked nervously. 'There's plenty of room.'

'Make a straight line!' a familiar voice boomed from behind the school wall, and out popped Miss Gauntlet. She was just like a spy.

'Thank goodness *she's* not coming,' Lugsy whispered in Monica's ear, as they scrambled aboard. 'Mr Simpkins is bad enough.'

'Oh I don't know . . .' she said thoughtfully, plopping down into a seat, with two bulging carrier bags. 'He's all right. He's just a bit frightened of us. Look, his hands have gone all trembly.'

Mr Simpkins was sitting at the front with the form genius, Clifford Biggs. He was the kind of boy who got ten out of ten for everything, and whose hand never went down in class. Monica said he slept with it stuck in the air. She called him Superswot. He was talking to Mr Simpkins about their new home computer.

It sounded very boring to Lugsy. Clifford was always boasting about something. His dad owned two factories and they'd got pots of money. He'd brought a five pound note with him on this school trip, Lugsy had seen it sticking out of his trouser pocket. He'd have to be careful. That money would be pinched if he didn't watch out. There were always thieves about in public places, and Superswot *looked* rich.

Lugsy stared glumly out of the window as the coach crawled through the traffic. At this rate they wouldn't get to Ramshaw's Zoo till closing time. Who wanted to go anyway? It was the most run-down place he'd ever seen, with a load of moth-eaten animals and a broken-down 'adventure playground'. What a place to choose for a school trip!

Monica called it *Ramshackle* Zoo, because it was.

'Is that *all* dinner?' he said, pointing at her two carrier bags. 'You look as if you've brought enough for the whole class.'

11

Monica giggled, and her round red face went even redder. 'I have. My mother made me. Look.'

One of the bags contained a large lunch-box, an anorak, and a brush for the big blonde busby. The other was full of oranges, all small and squishy-looking, with funny green patches. Lugsy wrinkled his nose. The oranges were very ripe, and the smell was filling the whole coach.

'I . . . what . . . *why bring all those?*' he spluttered. 'They're banned anyway.'

Monica glanced at Mr Simpkins and looked scornful. 'He won't even notice,' she said, 'and oranges are *good* for you. My mum says modern children don't get enough vitamins, so she sent these. They'd gone a bit too soft to sell in the shop. Here, have one.'

'Er, no thanks,' said Lugsy, shrinking away. He didn't like those suspicious green blotches. 'They're a funny colour,' he added.

'They're *organic*,' explained Monica. 'No false colouring. You could eat the peel as well, if you wanted to.'

Ugh. Lugsy went back to staring through the window. Nineteen organic oranges, to be eaten (with peel) at Ramshackle Zoo and Pleasure Grounds. It was going to be the trip of a lifetime.

Monica Teesdale was nosy, and she was busy going through the contents of Lugsy's rucksack. 'Syrup sandwiches,' she whispered in rapture. (He'd made them himself, at the last minute.) 'I'll swap you for these . . . *Cheese and onion crisps.* I'll – what will you swap for these?'

'*Not oranges,*' Lugsy said firmly, thinking of all that greenish-coloured peel.

'What's this?' she said suddenly.

'Give it here,' whispered Lugsy, and he pulled down his T-shirt to hide what she'd just discovered under the syrup sandwiches. It was a small black pistol, all shiny new, Lugsy's latest gun.

When she saw it Monica's eyes went all round and bulgy. It looked *real*.

'That could come in useful,' she said, in a breathless whisper. 'You might catch a thief with that. Or . . . or one of the animals might escape, and you could corner it. A lion or something. You never know.'

'Don't be daft,' grunted Lugsy. 'I bet Ramshaw's haven't got any lions. They eat too much. This gun's just for target practice, it shoots these.' And he dug down, into his pocket.

Monica watched as he slid a 'super rocket attack bullet' down the barrel. It was all red and floppy, with a flat sucker on the end. Lugsy licked it, aimed at the seat in front, and fired.

'Ping-g-g!' The bullet was firmly stuck to the seat, still whirring to and fro. It made a little sucking noise as Lugsy pulled it off.

'Great, isn't it?' he said, thrusting both gun and bullet deep into his pocket. 'Thought I might try it out in the open air, if we ever get there.'

Monica was looking dreamily at the little bald patch on the back of Mr Simpkins's head. She still fancied a chase, with Lugsy waving his gun, and some slippery criminal brought flat on his face and dragged off to prison.

But things like that didn't happen on their school trips. Someone being sick on the coach would be the biggest excitement.

'You'll have to be careful with that, Lugsy,' she murmured, still staring at Mr Simpkins's head. 'It could hurt someone.'

'I *know*,' replied Lugsy, a bit cross. 'I only meant at a tree, or something.' But in the dark of his pocket his finger was curled gently round the trigger. It was his best gun yet, he'd bought it with Uncle Norman's birthday money.

A cheer went up from the back as the coach turned into a drive-way and rumbled past a sign that said 'Ramshaw's Zoo and Pleasure Grounds'. Lugsy didn't even notice. He was thinking of Green End School and Miss Gauntlet, grimly picking up litter in the playground.

'No guns, no oranges.' That's what she'd said. And here they were, with both.

Baldilocks

As THEY CLIMBED off the coach it started to rain. Mr Simpkins made everyone wear anoraks, and gave out the school hats. Green End didn't have a uniform but on trips you had to wear a special hat in case you got lost. Blue for the boys and red for the girls. They were shapeless and floppy, and everyone hated them.

The tour began at 'Monkey Kingdom'. A big hairy chimpanzee looked down from a branch and screeched with laughter. From where he sat 3.S. looked like a row of big Smarties, all getting wet.

Ramshaw's Zoo was very boring, and worse in the drizzle. The big animals were all asleep and the little ones kept hiding in nests of straw. Superswot claimed he'd seen a zebra on the far side of a field, but it had vanished when the rest of 3.S. arrived.

The only creatures with any spark of life were two fat rabbits in 'Pets Corner'. The children pulled up handfuls of grass and dandelions and pushed them through the wire netting.

Lugsy watched the animals munching away, and felt miserable. His hat had turned into a soggy lump and there was water dripping down his neck. These two weren't a patch on *his* rabbit. It was called Bouncer and it could dribble a ping-pong ball. It also liked television.

Monica wasn't interested in the zoo either. Her hobby was watching people. She noticed how Superswot

sucked up to Mr Simpkins, and how the Nutter twins had slipped off to the 'Adventure Playground' the minute his back was turned.

'Terry! Neil!' he was soon yelling in panic. (He was terrified of losing someone.)

'In there,' Monica said calmly, 'crawling through the pipe.'

You'd have thought the Nutters had gone into orbit, the way Mr Simpkins went on at them, when their muddy faces popped out of that pipe. 'Now come *on*,' he shouted, grabbing them. 'It's time for dinner. You can play here afterwards.'

A man followed them into the picnic hut, a man Monica had been watching very carefully. He had a sly sort of face and a shiny bald head. He looked much too young to have lost all his hair, and she decided he must have shaved it all off. She christened him Baldilocks.

He didn't have a lunch box, and he didn't seem to be with anyone. He just sat on his own at a table, staring at them all, and chewing a Mars Bar. His sly shut-in face and crafty little

eyes gave Monica a funny cold feeling, all down her back.

Nobody wanted the oranges. She ate one herself and Melanie Andrews ate one, just to be polite. But the rest stayed at the bottom of the carrier bag, getting squishier and smellier, with juice dripping out of the corners. Monica wished she'd left them behind, on the coach.

Lugsy nearly got into trouble too, because of his gun. It fell out of his pocket as he bent down to pick something up off the floor, and Clifford Biggs spotted it.

'What've you brought that for, Lugsy?' he said, in a loud voice. 'Guns are banned, Miss Gauntlet said so.'

Clifford was a sneak as well as a swot, and it'd be just like him to tell Mr Simpkins.

'I brought it to play with,' muttered Lugsy, 'in case it turned wet.' (It *was* wet!) 'Keep your voice down, can't you?'

It would probably have ended up inside the Simpkins Zipper Bag along with three pen-knives, a pea-shooter, and six packets of bubble gum. But Superswot, feeling in his back pocket, suddenly let out an ear-splitting yell, and rushed up to the teacher. 'My money's gone, Sir!' he shrieked. 'From my jeans! *I've been robbed*!'

Mr Simpkins dropped the pork-pie he was eating and Lugsy quickly shoved the gun right to the bottom of his rucksack. 3.S. were called together and a search began. There were apple cores and peanuts and half-chewed sandwiches on the floor of the picnic hut, but no five pound note.

'Serves him right,' Monica whispered to Lugsy, as their faces met under a table. 'Maximum spending-money one pound. That's what Stone Age Woman said. He's just a show-off.'

'I'm sorry, Clifford,' said Mr Simpkins, brushing mouldy crisps off his trousers. 'You should have given *me* your money.' But Superswot's mouth had crumpled up, and he looked ready to cry.

'Spoiled,' muttered Monica into Lugsy's ear. 'It's his own fault, anyway.'

'It must have been a pick-pocket,'

25

Lugsy mumbled back, thinking of all the guns you could buy with five pounds. He felt a bit sorry for Superswot.

Meanwhile, Monica's sharp eyes were skinning the picnic hut for Baldilocks. He'd been there when 3.S. had dived under the tables, gone when they'd come out again.

'I think I know who did it,' she said quietly, peeling another orange (three down and sixteen to go). 'It was a man with a bald head. He kept staring at us.'

'But you can't say he's a thief, just because he stared,' Lugsy pointed out. 'That's not fair.'

'He took it, I know he did. I feel it in my *bones*,' said Monica mysteriously.

Lugsy didn't argue after that, but he too began to look round for the man with the bald head. He'd heard about Monica's *bones* before, and he had great respect for them.

Superman Simpkins

IT WAS POURING down now, so they couldn't go to the Adventure Playground. Instead, they all trooped into the Gift Shop, to spend their money.

Lugsy got a purple plastic dinosaur, and Monica bought a fluffy white rabbit to sit on her dressing table, with all the brushes and combs. The Nutters bought The Hardest Jigsaw in

the World, to drive their mother mad. They were crazy about jigsaws.

Superswot moped about, not buying anything. Then Mr Simpkins lent him a pound, and he spent it all on sweets. '*See*', said Monica, 'he's quite kind underneath. It's Miss Gauntlet who makes him so bad-tempered. *She* wouldn't have done that.'

She watched enviously as Superswot gobbled his way through a great big chocolate bar. The oranges were getting heavier and heavier, and juice had dripped all over her white socks. She'd given up offering them round, they were turning into a slimy mess now.

The Gift Shop was full of school parties and their coaches were lined up outside, waiting to go home. But 3.S.'s driver wasn't coming back for another hour, and to round off the day Miss Gauntlet had laid on a talk about elephants.

Elephants. They all went through a glass door into a special 'talks area' and sat on hard benches while an old man mumbled at them. He looked like an elephant himself, with his long droopy nose, his big flopping ears and his grey crumpled face.

Lugsy thought an elephant might have nicked Superswot's five pounds, with its trunk. But the animals at Ramshaw's were too dim for that.

Monica was right at the end of the back bench, and she could see through to the Gift Shop. The person who'd served them, a young woman with glasses and a blue overall, was counting her money now, and putting it into little plastic bags. There was the chink of coin and the crackle of paper, as she added up her 'takings' for the day.

A 'Closed' notice swung on the locked door, but the shop wasn't empty. Someone was in there, skulking around, someone whose round bald head gleamed pinkly under the electric light.

Baldilocks!

Monica stiffened, and prodded Lugsy. All 3.S.'s bags and rucksacks had been left outside the 'talks area', by order of the elephant man, and Baldilocks was busy, going through them.

'Hey! He's got my gun!' muttered Lugsy. 'Well of all the –'

'*Shut up!*' Monica hissed. She was nudging the glass door open with her foot, pushing him through.

Nobody noticed. Blinds had been pulled down now, and the old man was showing slides. 'This old chap could live seventy years,' he was saying. 'He eats no meat, of course, just leaves and fruit. But look at the *size* of him, boys and girls. . . .'

But overweight elephants meant nothing to Lugsy and Monica. Baldilocks was at the till now, looming over the woman with the glasses. She looked petrified. His left hand was stuffing all the little money bags down inside his zipper jacket, his right hand held the toy gun to her head.

Under the strip light the little black pistol shone horribly, and her face was grey with terror. Lugsy looked from the gun to the till, then to Baldilocks, and felt sick.

Then Monica opened her mouth. She had a voice that shattered glass and she'd been banned from school choir on Day One. 'Mr Simpkins!' she shrieked, *'Mr Simpkins!!!'* And as the bewildered teacher appeared in the doorway she dived through his spindly legs and made a grab for her carrier bags.

Superman Simpkins summed it all up in seconds. He seemed to grow a foot taller, his chest swelled out, and in a voice That Must Be Obeyed he bellowed *'Drop that gun! The police are outside!'* Then he hurtled across the Gift Shop towards the till,

scattering post-cards and plastic kangaroos and key-rings as he went.

It didn't matter. Nothing mattered except saving the poor trembling shop woman from Baldilocks, and rescuing the day's takings, and getting back Superswot's five pounds. It was quite obvious where *that* had gone.

But Baldilocks was making for the door. Mr Simpkins had wrenched Lugsy's gun from the man's hand, and it went clattering to the floor, too fast for the teacher to realise that it was only a toy. But Baldilocks still had all the money bags.

'Quick!' yelled Monica, opening her carrier. 'We can't let him get away now.'

Lugsy was a very good shot (his guns had given him a lot of practice). *Splat!* The first orange hit Baldilocks

between the eyes. *Squish!* The second
landed inside his collar and all the
juice dripped down, over his hairy
chest. *Thung!* The third landed
between his teeth. His mouth had
dropped open in sheer amazement

when the oranges started coming, and
Lugsy threw dead straight. But the
man wasn't beaten yet, he'd managed
to undo all the bolts and he was
tugging at the main door.

Superman Simpkins had vanished
under the counter. At the sight of that
gun the poor woman with glasses had
fainted with shock and he was on his
knees, fanning her with a paper bag.
Then, just behind her head, he saw a

red 'Emergency Alarm' button.

The minute he pressed it bells started ringing, all over the place.

Oranges and Guns

ON THE OTHER side of the counter there was a deafening crash, then a tinkle of breaking china and a roar of pain. While Baldilocks was tugging at the door Monica had dived into her carrier bag and had started hurling oranges across the floor, aiming at the man's feet.

The Gift Shop was tiled with shiny plastic squares. Baldilocks skidded as he tried to get away, slithering and skating about as his heavy boots finally disappeared from under him. He did the splits as he hit the floor, collapsing in a mess of pips, pulp and soggy peel. Nobody would have bought those oranges at Teesdales' Health Store but for catching crooks there was nothing better.

Huddled round the doorway of the 'talks area' 3.S. cheered loudly. 'Adult height, 305 centimetres, Habitat, Sub Tropical Forest. . . .' The old man droned on and on, but no one was listening any more. They were far too interested in what was happening next door. It was better than James Bond.

Suddenly Mr Simpkins's head appeared from under the cash desk. He was pulling the shopwoman to her feet now, and sitting her down on a stool.

At the same moment the shop door

burst open and in rushed two Ramshaw Park Rangers in tatty green uniforms. They were big and red-cheeked and weighed thirty stone between them, and they towered over Baldilocks as he sat there on the floor.

He really was a pathetic sight, with orange juice dribbling down his chin, and the remains of twenty china elephants scattered all round him. He'd broken a whole shelf of the things as he tried to escape.

'Going somewhere, were you?' said a sneery little voice. Baldilocks looked up miserably. Standing between the two hefty Park Rangers was a small neat man in a checked suit, puffing on a fat cigar. It was the Boss, Alfred Ramshaw himself, the Brains behind Ramshackle Zoo and Pleasure Grounds.

When he heard the full story he couldn't do enough for 3.S. The police arrived in five minutes flat and carted Baldilocks away. The takings went into the safe, and Superswot even got his five pounds back. Then they were all treated to hot dogs and chips at the cafeteria, before going home.

Monica and Lugsy had to sit with Mr Simpkins, and he kept telling them how proud he was, and how proud Miss Gauntlet would be. (Not a word about the oranges. Not a whisper about the gun.)

It was funny, but Lugsy didn't want the gun any more. On the coach he decided to give it to his little brother, Eddie, when they got back. It was when Baldilocks had threatened the poor shopwoman with it, when everyone thought it was real. He'd suddenly gone right off guns.

Monica hadn't gone off eating though. She'd had three hot dogs in the cafeteria, and two Cokes, and half a ton of chips. Now she was sucking oranges. There'd been a few left over, at the bottom of the bag.

'Want some orange, Mr Simpkins?'
she called out, tapping him on the
shoulder. (Clifford Biggs was being
boring again, about his home
computer.)

Superman turned round and
grinned. 'Thanks, Monica,' he said, 'I
don't mind if I do.'

And he took a very large slice.